Lost Pe

Also by Margaret Elphinstone

The Incomer (1987)
A Sparrow's Flight (1989)
Outside Eden (1990)
An Apple from a Tree (1991)
Islanders (1994)
The Sea Road (2000)
Hy Brasil (2002)
Voyageurs (2003)
Gato (2005)
Light (2006)
The Gathering Night (2009)

Lost People

Margaret Elphinstone

wild goose publications   www.ionabooks.com

Copyright © Margaret Elphinstone 2023

First published 2024 by
Wild Goose Publications
Suite 9, Fairfield
1048 Govan Road, Glasgow G51 4XS, Scotland
A division of Iona Community Trading CIC
Limited Company Reg. No. SC156678
www.ionabooks.com

ISBN 978-1-80432-317-5

Cover drawing of 'Cosette' by Frances Robertson
Cover composition by Wild Goose Publications

All rights reserved. No part of this publication may be reproduced in any form or by any means, including photocopying or any information storage or retrieval system, without written permission from the publisher via PLSclear.com.

Margaret Elphinstone has asserted her right in accordance with the Copyright, Designs and Patents Act, 1988, to be identified as the author of this work.

Overseas distribution
Australia: Willow Connection Pty Ltd, 1/13 Kell Mather Drive, Lennox Head NSW 2478
New Zealand: Pleroma, Higginson Street, Otane 4170, Central Hawkes Bay

Printed in the UK by Page Bros (Norwich) Ltd

Contents

1   Sanctuary   9

2   Duets   25

3   Maze   45

4   Solace   65

For all the Lost People

One

Sanctuary

Thyme is delicate. You take each little stalk and rub the leaves off backwards. Then pinch out the tuft at the top between your fingernails. It's easier when the stalks have dried. I sit on the curved step, and as the day passes I shift around the sundial, sitting in its shadow. The air is heavy with herb-smells. My basket slowly fills. I sift thyme and write my story in counterpoint. Each is a rest from the other.

I don't know how long I've been here. It was winter when we arrived, and almost summer when she left. The years go by.

She told me she was leaving, but I didn't understand.

After she'd gone I flitted from place to place looking for somewhere warm. The knot garden catches the sun and holds it, just as it holds me. The knot garden was all I had, but when the sun goes down there is nowhere to be. I went indoors, a little frightened shadow stepping between tall doorways. The stone floors of the passages were cold on the soles of my feet. I stood in the middle of the hall. Carved oak panels dissolved high in the twilight. An oak staircase with a carved gryphon at the end of the bannister curled out of my sight. Perhaps it was warm up there. Somehow I knew that was where the Nunks lived. I wasn't afraid of them but I knew there was a boundary on that stair I could not break.

Very quietly I opened one of the heavy doors that lined the hall. The darkness smelt of books and wood ash. Safe walls enclosed a well-inhabited emptiness. It was warm. I closed the door carefully and felt my way with my hands held out in front of me. I saw embers glowing. By their faint light I found a big chair with a cushion and a rug. It smelt of leather and of someone old and kind. I wrapped myself up. The firelight comforted me. I was asleep before it faded.

I couldn't always sleep on the Library chair because sometimes the Nunks stayed up late. If that happened I made a nest for myself behind the heavy curtain. It was cold by the window, but the Nunks' rustlings and occasional murmurings were comforting in a different way. Sometimes there was too much light in the Library for me to slip in unseen. I had to look elsewhere, but every other place was very cold. The Refectory smelt of old dinners. I slept there once, wrapped in a green baize tablecloth. The floor was hard.

I found my way back to the Supplicants' Wing, where she and I had stayed when we arrived. The Supplicants' bookroom was warm and had soft sofas, but I wasn't at peace there. Supplicants come and go. You can't be sure what they will do. Sometimes they rummage in the bookroom at night, or wander up and down the stairs with cups of tea. The Supplicants' Wing is weighted with inexplicable emotions. I didn't want to meet the Supplicants. They never saw me.

When the Orphans played in the woods they never looked up. I could easily have spat on one of their heads. The thought made me smile as I lay along a branch, pressing my cheek against rough oak bark. The Orphans lived across the courtyard, above the stables. I always knew when they weren't in school because they screamed like the gulls who come upriver when it's stormy. I could hear them as far away as the knot garden. Sometimes the Orphans kicked a ball up and down the grass; sometimes they fought each other, rolling over and over down the bank, always screaming. Sometimes they huddled in small groups with their heads almost touching. They had their own Providers, one of whom used to come out at regular intervals and swing a big bell. The bell had a pleasing resonance, and better still, when it rang, the discordance ceased and the Orphans trooped indoors.

Caleb came to me long before I found Phyllis. Caleb was also a wanderer looking for warmth and food. There were things we could give one another. I could open the Library door, which Caleb could not. No one else ever heard me open it but Caleb always did. We would share the big armchair and the cushions. Caleb kneaded my thin shirt and purred in my face, dribbling a little in his ecstasy. When we lay close I could feel him breathe, and that made me breathe more easily too.

I learned from Caleb how to be invisible. Caleb could slip across to the hearthrug at the very feet of the Nunks, and curl up in front of their eyes. They were too deep in their books and conversations to notice. I copied Caleb, and found I could do the same, just as no one noticed when I slipped into the Refectory at mealtimes. On some days the Nunks and Supplicants eat there together. No one knows everybody and that made it easy. Other days I hung around the trolleys in the pantry, and one of the Providers would slip me a full plate. But it was cold eating in the pantry, which is really just a corridor between the Kitchens and the Refectory. I grew bolder, and began to draw up my chair at the long table among the Nunks, even on days when the Supplicants were eating and talking in their own dining room. The Nunks eat in silence, listening to the Reader. The Reader tells wonderful stories. Sometimes I understood them, sometimes not. Sometimes they were in my language, and other times not. But all the stories and languages were beautiful, and the less I could understand the words, the more

I was enchanted by the colours of the sounds.

Phyllis got used to seeing me hovering in the pantry. She fed Caleb every day, and she began to make sure I was fed too. She saw how I lived like a little shadow, always seeking warmth. The days were getting shorter. One grey afternoon the rain fell so consistently I couldn't go into the knot garden at all. I stood shivering at the pantry window looking down at the sodden quadrangles. Water coursed down the window-pane, not even separate drops but a whole shimmering sheet so the quadrangles looked blurred as if they were moving.

Phyllis said, "Come with me."

I followed her warily. The corridors in this part of the house were lower. We walked on brown matting which tickled my feet. There were high windows and many closed doors. Phyllis opened the door at the end.

The noise hit me like a hammer. My hands flew to shield my head. I turned to flee, but the door slammed shut.

"Keep that door shut! It's freezing out there! What's this? Who is it? Where did you find it?"

"All in good time,' said Phyllis. "This child is cold and hungry." She turned to me. "Don't be frightened. We're just some of the Providers. You can sit at the table – that side – you'll be nearer the fire."

I slipped round the table, and there was Caleb on the mat by the hearth. My insides stopped trembling. Presently I was able to raise my eyes from my empty plate and look at all the people, even though it was so noisy. They never stopped talking and crashing dishes, but no one took any notice of me. There were actually only four of them. I sat on my wooden chair and felt the heat of the fire on my back. I could smell rosemary and sage, and potatoes roasting. Even when Phyllis left the room I stayed where I was.

After a while she came back with a big bundle in her arms. She jerked her head towards me, "Come!"

This time we went down a narrow flight of stairs. Through the window at the bottom I saw the knot garden, right on our level. There was a door with a big key in it which opened straight on to it. I must have smiled.

"Yes, I see you in the knot garden every day. That's your place, isn't it?"

I looked at her. So she'd been watching me.

"My name's Phyllis," she told me. "Do you have a name?"

I turned over in my mind why she might be asking. Then I nodded.

Phyllis waited for a moment, and then she said, "Well, that's good. Now look, if you're going to live among us you must have somewhere to sleep. Everyone who lives here has their own bed, where they can rest. But you're not a Supplicant, so you can't have a place there any more. You're not an Orphan, we know that. You're certainly not a Nunk – that's a joke, by the way. I don't suppose you do jokes? – And you're not a Provider because you don't do anything for anybody. So I thought about where you could go, and see here … I found the answer."

We went through a door on the right into a broad passage lined with wooden casks on one side and windows on to the knot garden on the other. "See this door – that's the lavatory. A proper old-fashioned flushing toilet. All yours. No one else'll use it outside working hours. You're not a cat, so you can stop behaving like one. Keep that door closed. Now, in here."

She held the next door open for me to go in first.

It was warm. Big round pipes lined the walls. White sheets hung like sails from high pulleys. Racks of towels, pillow slips, cloths, shirts, underwear, trousers, long lines of coloured socks. Huge white sinks with brass taps, and shining tanks. "Here!" A clothes horse covered with a brightly-woven blanket shielded the far corner under the pipes. "I made you a bed, see. Mattress, sheet, pillow, plenty of blankets. That's a rag rug for your cold feet in the morning. No one will disturb you behind here. I've told them not to. It's your own."

I think I gave Phyllis a smile. I hope I did. I hadn't felt so happy for a long time.

"Clothes," Phyllis was still talking. "Winter's coming on. You'll need warm clothes. Outdoor things if you want to be in the knot garden. Boots. I got these from the Orphans' store. No one will miss them. Here, let me measure them against your feet."

I backed away.

"Don't be silly, I'm not going to touch you. I'll leave the things here. You can dress yourself?"

I nodded indignantly.

"So I should hope. And that's another thing. Washing. You're not Caleb; you can't lick yourself clean. See these sinks? Hot tap, under the tank there. Cold tap, here. 'H' for 'hot', 'C' for cold, if you can read. There's always hot water in the morning. You'll need to be finished before breakfast; there'll be Providers in here most mornings. Soap, see? Flannel. Nice clean towel. You know what to do?"

Each night I lay in the velvety dark and smelled clean clothes airing around me. Caleb often shared my lair. He had other places too. That was all right because I also had other places inside my mind. The scent of aired cloth struck a note which echoed deep within me, far below where my waking mind could follow. It was like the warmth of Caleb against my heart, feeling his soft breath. Something held me from long ago, but I couldn't call it back, not when I was awake. The patterns on the woven blanket that draped my clothes horse were in quadrangles like the knot garden, intricate and angular, a maze of possibilities in vibrant colours: red, ochre, yellow, gold. When summer came I opened the window so when I lay in bed I could smell the herbs in my knot garden. As I defined each smell I'd see in my mind's eye how it looked and where it grew: sage, thyme, garlic, hyssop, mint, rosemary, sorrel, marjoram … I was always asleep before I'd got to the end of the quadrangle.

After a while Sister Angela allocated the first quadrangle to me, closest to the laundry window. "You can't just haunt the place," she told me. "While we breathe we're here to be of use. The first thing is to learn their names."

She was wrong, it hadn't been the first thing, but I was pleased to learn them now. When she realised I could read quite long words, she gave me a book with pictures of all the herbs. Under each one was a description of its properties and applications. I studied it every day, sitting on the sundial steps when it was fine, or on the laundry windowsill when it rained. From both places I could survey the knot garden, and think about what my plants needed even as I read.

The knot pattern was older than the herbs that inhabited it. In the beginning, long before Sister Angela was born, the four quadrangles were all alike, with box hedges and gravel paths and nothing in between. Over the years the angular spaces were filled with plants, reflecting how ideas changed and what people needed most. As long as these people, whom Sister Angela seemed to mind about even when she didn't know who they were, didn't come into my garden I didn't care what they needed. But when Sister Angela talked about the plants and the insects who rely upon one another to survive, and about the birds who sang their hearts out all around us through the sunny days, I listened to her stories with all my might. I listened as well to the thrush, the blackbird, the robin and the wren, and all the other bird-voices raised in concert round me, never a note out of place, saying all that they needed to say and nothing more.

Between the box hedges that shaped my quadrangle, at the beginning I found lavender, rosemary, southernwood, thyme and a bay tree where the four squares met. I learned to take slips and grow more. I cut them back at the end of summer and dried the trimmings in the laundry. Some of my harvest went to the Kitchen, some to the Apothecary. In autumn I collected seeds to sow again in spring. Sometimes they bred true, sometimes not, and as the seasons passed I began to work out why. My sleeping place was redolent of lavender which brings repose, rosemary for remembrance, southernwood for feeling safe and having good dreams, thyme to help you breathe, bay for flavouring and protecting your mind. As more seasons passed I started to bring in other herbs from the woods and fields around. The Supplicants got to hear that herbs were wanted in the garden, and sometimes they used to bring plants when they visited. In my one quadrangle I ended up with thirty-two herbs. My favourites? Borage, bluer than the summer sky, which cures your melancholy and stops you going mad. Sweet cicely, sorrel and summer savoury for subtle tastes, mint, garlic, sage and chives for strong ones. Parsley for strength through sickness, rue for purging and making you pure. Wormwood, which I first grew as a specific against clothes moths, I love almost the most because it reminds you that life is sweet because it is so bitter.

Several times a day, while I worked, the sound of human singing, and sometimes magical notes not made by any human voice, wafted over to the knot garden. To begin with I had no idea what it could be. I used to pause in my work to listen. It was resonant like the bees; in the same way it thrilled me through. It had always been there, but only in the peace of my work did I really start to hear it. The day came when I laid down my hand hoe and walked quietly towards the source. I left the knot garden by the eastern arch and crossed the orchard. I recognised the building; I'd seen it from the other side. This was where the Nunks went for Practice.

There was a little door in the wall. I slipped inside. The place was cold and vast. When I looked up the ceiling was so far away I seemed to see clouds obscuring it. The walls were white. The huge space felt profoundly empty. I would have fled, but there, right in the middle, tiny under the soaring arches, little figures were moving. Their presence was bright and warm. And yet, when I looked again, it was just the Nunks in their shapeless old jerseys standing or sitting in a ragged circle. The brightness was actually the music. The Nunks were singing with all their different voices, from the highest through to the lowest, so that all together they made one glorious sound, the kind that breaks your heart wide open. Others were playing instruments. The clouds seemed to clear so I could pick out the different ones. From somewhere way back inside my mind I recognised a flute, a cello, a violin. Such beautiful colours, weaving and swirling, joining together and soaring away again. All the colours I'd ever seen, like all the different herbs in a garden, making a pattern which, if only I could see the whole of it, would at last make sense.

The celandines were out, and the woods reeking of wild garlic, when the time came for the Nunks to talk about me. Phyllis told the Providers at tea break. They were sitting round the kitchen table, and I was behind the larder door stealing a jam tart, so I heard about it. I knew what I had to do. The Meetings Room has few places to hide, but I made myself small under one of the carved benches at the back. The stone wall behind me had green patches and smelt of damp. The underneath of the bench hadn't been properly varnished; you could see the drip marks. I waited a long time before the Nunks came in, and it was an even longer time before they started talking about me. Their voices droned like creaky violins, on and on. I thought how still Caleb could keep when he was hunting, and I did the same.

"So how long has this child been here?"

This was me! For a moment I stopped breathing.

"She came …"

"*He.*"

"I'm sorry?"

"Isn't it a boy? I'm sure I've seen a boy."

"No, it's a girl. At least …"

"I thought …"

"Does it matter?" That was Sister Angela. I already knew she was wise. "It doesn't affect anything. Or do you think it does?"

There was a short silence.

"What's her – his – its – name? Do we know that?"

"Does that affect anything either?" asked Sister Angela.

"The point is," – this voice was more cello than violin – "its mother came as a Supplicant, and stayed as long as the rule allowed. She left when she had to, and no one realised until she'd disappeared that she'd left the child behind."

"Basically, she abandoned it."

"Perhaps she did it for the best," – Sister Angela again – "Would she have had anywhere to go? We know all too well why the Supplicants come. She must have thought the child would be safer here."

"Brother Anthony, you said you remembered the woman?"

"I had Care of the Supplicants while she was here."

"What mother abandons her child, not knowing ..."

"Was she its mother?"

"How wouldn't she be?"

Brother Anthony spoke double bass, which fitted. Brother Anthony really did play double bass at Practice. "The child isn't remotely like her. This woman was White – white skin, pale blonde hair, green eyes – utterly White. The child is more ordinary, a mix, I'd say."

"That tells us nothing. We have no idea who the father may have been."

"Does this affect anything?" In this performance, Sister Angela clearly held the refrain. "I thought we were here to discuss what we're going to do with it. The child is neither a Supplicant – it's been here too long for that – nor an Orphan, because she's not come from a War Zone through the usual arrangements. He can't be a Provider – he's too young to work.

Shouldn't we be thinking about its education?"

"What I'd like to know is" – this was a new voice, clear as a flute – "what does the child think should happen?"

"The child says nothing."

"Has anyone asked it?"

"You don't understand. I mean exactly what I say. The child says nothing. It doesn't speak."

"Dear me," said a placid elderly voice, as if a person's silence didn't matter in the least. "Is this due to a lack of linguistic capability, morbid laziness, or some previous trauma?"

"The child's intelligent all right," said Sister Angela sharply. She sounded angry. Could this be on my behalf? "Eager to learn, and very clever with the herbs."

Cramped against the damp wall, I felt a glow inside me, like being right up close to the Library fire on a wintry night.

"If this child is intelligent, unhappy and quite alone in the world, I think it's clear where our duty lies." I knew that voice from Practice. It was actually the Conductor speaking. About me. I held my breath. "We must nurture it, heal it as far as we can, and educate it to the best of our ability. Thereby some have entertained angels unawares. Sister Angela, this child has, I understand, found sanctuary in the knot garden. Therefore you will continue to nurture it there. After all, herbs are for healing. As for education, we already have comprehensive provision on our premises. It must go to school with the Orphans."

"Will our donors consent? This isn't a War Orphan!"

"It may be, for all we know. It's a child in need. I've seen it myself. It warms itself on the Library hearthrug sometimes. It's quite small. It wouldn't take up much room on the end of a bench. No Orphan will lose a place because of it, and I don't think our donors could possibly object. Especially if they remain ignorant of it."

In spite of my terror, not everything at school was bad. I liked geometry, botany, music and logic. Geology was interesting but difficult. History made me sad. Literature was hard; the words were too slippery. Some of our teachers were Nunks, some were Providers. Each had advantages and disadvantages. None of the lessons bothered me as long as I could sit near the open window and not too far from the door. And as long as the Provider didn't leave the room.

The first time it happened the racket took me completely by surprise. Screaming, desk-banging, stamping, paper missiles flying across the room. I buried my head in my arms, my hands over my ears. Suddenly it was over, as the Provider walked back into the room. He shouted at us all. I hid my trembling deep inside. Only one person noticed.

Days passed before he spoke to me. He sat next to me; he'd had to move up a few inches, but he was thin too, and I didn't take up any more room than I had to.

He said, "I'm Basil by the way. What's your name?"

Basil is the King of Herbs. It's mostly used in cooking, but it's also a specific against the deadly cancers that eat you up from the inside. Basil is tasteful and kindly. Basil didn't mind me not answering. Nor did he mind that I never stayed to play when the bell rang, but ran away to the knot garden until the bell rang again to tell me it was time for class. He didn't seem to mind anything about me. He was an Orphan and lived a different life, always with other people. He had many friends. I got used to him sitting so close to me. He had no choice, because there wasn't really enough room on the bench. The herb basil has a flavoursome tangy smell; the boy had a similar sort of character, nothing mean about him.

One day he pulled my spelling notebook towards him. The Orphans do things like that quite casually, as if they all belong to one another. I resisted the impulse to snatch it back.

"You can write, anyway. Why don't you talk? In fact, look, you write better than I do. That's really good. Tell you what. You could write down what you want me to call you. I need to call you something if we're going to be friends. Write it here."

If we're going to be friends? I didn't know what he meant. The Orphans had friends, with whom they fought or kicked balls or ran shouting along the woodland paths. I thought of my quiet quadrangle in the knot garden, which Sister Angela had given me for my own. I thought of Caleb. Of Phyllis. Of Sister Angela. None of them were like this boy Basil. Basil's eyes, when we sat on the bench next to each other, were exactly on a level with mine. Brown eyes, with black centres. I could see right into them without having to look up or down. For some reason this seemed significant.

I thought for a long time. Then I slid my notebook back. I took my pen and wrote. I handed it to him so he could read it.

I'd written, in my best lettering, "You can call me RUE."

Two

Duets

I said, "It isn't *about* anything. I don't want to explain."

"But you explained about the herbs. You know all their stories. You told me them."

"The first quadrangle *needed* explaining. This is the *second* quadrangle. Colours. They don't *mean* anything."

"But they do. They're all in a pattern. I can see that."

"Of course they are."

"So what's the idea of the pattern?"

I found myself explaining, whether I liked it or not, making shapes with my hands in the air. No one tried to make me talk in straight lines any more; everyone knew I spoke in angles. "One way you look at it, like *this*" – I drew an imaginary vertical line – "Red, ochre, yellow, gold: snapdragon, marigold, daisies, nasturtium. Lavender is *counterpoint*. The other way – "I drew a horizontal line in the air – "Seasons in *layers*, like sedimentary rocks. It began with aconite, crocus, anemone … then sweet-scented wallflower, primrose, narcissus … and now summer. Box edges all year round of course. For *contrast*."

"A graph is a story too."

"No, not a story. A *pattern*. This is the *second* quadrangle."

"Fair enough." Basil always said this when he gave up. "Sit down. I want to tell you something."

We sat on the shady side of the sundial step. I said, "The flowers aren't *perennials*. Other seasons, it'll be *different* … Depends what happens … "

"That's what I want to talk about."

"No point talking about colours. You *can't*. Describe me a colour. Tell me the difference between orange and yellow. Can you make it into words? No, you can't. That's the whole point."

"Stop it. You're doing it on purpose. You've got to let me tell you."

I stared at the bay tree in the first quadrangle.

"Rue," said Basil, "I'm going away."

My first thought was, so who's going to cut my hair?

All the Orphans were taught when they arrived how to cut each other's hair, so that together they could be as independent as possible. I'd let Basil cut off my grubby tangles a long time ago. I felt so light when it was done: no more lice, no more itching, no more Providers brandishing scissors trying to corner me. The feel of cool air round my ears and neck, a long-forgotten lightness that reminded me of something else I couldn't catch hold of. I could cut my own hair now if I had to; I needn't care if Basil abandoned me. I'd always known he would.

"I'm going to tell you why, and where. As far as I know, anyway."

It wasn't as if we were always together. Basil had his own life among the Orphans, so unlike mine that I couldn't begin to imagine it. The first time – long ago now – he'd shown me where the boy Orphans slept, I'd felt, even though the room was empty, as if I had to stop breathing. The Dormitory had once been a hayloft. It ran the whole length of the stables below. Two big windows, which had once been the hayloft doors, opened on to the yard, twelve feet above the ground. Our footsteps sounded soft, enclosed by woodenness: rough oak beams, planked roof and pine floor. The roof came down to the eaves. The ridge was so low that a tall boy could have touched it. The Orphans' mattresses, rolled up neatly against the sloping walls, were very close together. If an Orphan stretched out his arm at night, either side, he'd touch another Orphan. Anyone sleeping here would have to share his breathing with all the other boys round him, squeezed in together like fledglings in a nest. I shuddered.

Each boy had a box of his own, tucked under the eaves beside his mattress. Basil had a few books in his, a pair of slippers, a penknife, and some withered conkers. But this was long ago; he must have different treasures now. He had no clothes of his own; none of the Orphans did. He kept his shoes for as long as they fitted, and then he had to swap them for bigger ones from the store. Clean clothes were handed out on Saturdays by the Provider.

"We all help each other anyway," Basil had said suddenly, as if I had asked him something. "Unless anyone's really mean. Sometimes they come here like that, but almost always it gets better."

I had no idea what he meant. I often didn't, but that never mattered, because he knew I wasn't going to answer. The day I did answer, I really did surprise him.

I never went to singing. The Orphans' singing hurt my ears, and I always ran away. The winter came when we got our musical instruments. One by one we were sent to Brother Anselm to make our choice. I watched each Orphan called out of class, and after a while come back again, usually smiling. I didn't think they would call on me. But last of all, I was sent for too.

Brother Anselm was in the music room surrounded by violins of different sizes, two pianos, a rack of wind instruments, and a double bass in the far corner.

Brother Anselm played eight notes on the piano, like a staircase, one after the other, perfectly spaced. "Do you know what that is?"

I shook my head.

"You don't sing, I hear?"

I shook my head.

"Do you like singing? Do you ever sing by yourself?"

I stared at him.

"Come here." He beckoned me to the piano. "Would you like to learn music? Do you want to play one of these instruments?"

I nodded.

"You can have one if you have the ear to tune it. Let's see what you can do. I'm going to play a note, and you repeat it. Sing it, with your voice."

It was the first of the eight notes he'd just played. I thought of the Nunks, and the colours that turned the cold Practice Hall as bright as flame. I thought about the eight notes, two for each quadrangle, the pattern as regular as the steps of the oak staircase which led into the dimness where the Nunks live.

"Listen, I'll play it again. You sing: La...a."

He didn't need to play it again. I knew exactly what it was. Eight steps to the first landing, twice round the four paths enclosing the knot garden.

I trod the first step, I sang "La...a."

Brother Anselm looked at me under his brows. He played all the way up to the first landing. Eight steps. I sang my way after him. I wanted a musical instrument. I wanted, desperately, to get to the top of those stairs.

"Rue," Basil broke right across my thought. "Are you listening to me? This is important, what I'm telling you."

I blinked at him. Sitting there in the shadow of the sundial, I suddenly saw how he'd changed. You don't always notice when things happen slowly. "I was thinking about when Brother Anselm gave me my flute."

"Rue, that's nothing to do with what I'm talking about!"

"Yes it *is* or I wouldn't have thought of it."

"Rue, do you want to know where I'm going?"

What a stupid question. He'd been my friend for a long time; I didn't want anything to change.

"Well, if you don't, I want to tell you anyway. You've been my friend for a long time. That means one of the things you have to do is listen."

I knew that; he'd told me so often enough. I listened.

"I'm a War Orphan," said Basil. "Otherwise I wouldn't be here. I came the usual way. We're the lucky ones. When we get to sixteen or thereabouts, they let us read our own reports. I was found in a ruined village in the foothills – you know, where the border is, along the high ridge of the mountains. We've done it in geography, but then of course I didn't know that's where I came from. On my report it asks for age, and someone's written '3? 4?'"

"What do you remember?" I hadn't intended to ask questions, but for some reason this seemed important.

Basil hesitated, his eyes narrowed as if he were trying to make out movements on a distant hill. "Goats." A pause. "There were goats."

My turn to prompt him, which was unusual. "What colour goats?"

"White, I think. No, maybe brown. Their bells rang, coming down the hill."

"What did the bells sound like?"

Basil turned his face away. It was hard to make out what he was saying, "They sounded always the same. As if everything were always the same. As if it wouldn't change. Ever."

In the Providers' potting shed where we keep our tools and have our tea breaks when it rains, someone once painted green words in a flourishing script along the end partition. The writing was faded when I'd first read it, but anyone could still make it out: NOTHING IS FOREVER.

I was looking at it in my mind's eye when Basil started talking again. "Before I was a War Orphan there were two of us. I was the biggest. I think there was a baby too, but sometimes I think I've made up the baby. Or was it someone else's baby? We had Mum and Dad. Those were their names. Mum and Dad. Or did I make them up later? Sometimes I think I did. I can't see what they looked like. Maybe I did make them up. I need to find out."

"If you're a War Orphan, your parents must both be dead. That's in the rules."

"The report says I was the only one they found alive in that whole village. They burned the bodies. They couldn't dig a grave because the hill ground was so stony and there were too many to bury. That's what it says."

"You don't remember that part?"

"Jolting. Like jolting over a stony road, on and on. Not being able to see out. But maybe that was just a dream. Still is, sometimes. Never mind that. Rue, I know my family must all be dead. But I need to see the place for myself. I need to ask, find

out who they were, what their names were. I need to go there."
"Will you come back?"
"I don't know." Basil got up suddenly. "Rue, I have to go now. I'll say goodbye before I leave. I can't ... I have to go."
He fairly ran through the south archway, out of the knot garden and out of sight.

I decided to eat dinner with the Providers. On fine summer days they ate outside under the apple trees, the kitchen doors wide open behind them. I seldom joined them in winter because they chattered like a flock of starlings in a kiln, the noise swirling crazily round their low-beamed dining room. But in summer the blue sky swallowed up the sound, and apple leaves dappled us as we sat at the loaded tables. The Providers always ate well. They were the ones who grew the food and cooked it, and so they noticed what they ate. The Nunks took more interest in listening to the Reader, or at breakfast, where most of them usually spent at least an hour, they read their own books – they each had their own little bookstand with their name on it – and drank copious cups of tea. "Pearls before swine," Dennis used to say as he laid the steaming casseroles on the Refectory trolley. Dennis was one of the Cooks. I got to know him because he came to the knot garden every morning to pick fresh herbs. Dennis always said he knew by the weather where he would find me eating that day. I never, ever, went to the Orphans' dining room. I liked the dignified order of both Nunks and Providers. I enjoyed the piquant contrast between the two. With either I knew for certain I would be left in peace.

Today we had one of Dennis's goulashes followed by cherry

pie. The Providers got up one by one, cleared their plates, and sauntered back to work. I was still there when Dennis came back with two brimming cups and put one down in front of me. A little tea slopped over on to the table. I wiped it away with my sleeve. I knew Dennis was going to talk to me. I felt a pang in my stomach in spite of the comforting dinner inside it.

When everyone had the measles, it was Dennis who'd scooped me up from the sundial steps and carried me to the Sick Room because my legs were so wobbly. He held me as if I were just another basket of logs, and that made me feel safe. The strange feeling was being too weak to protest. Dennis kicked open the Sick Room door. "Here's another, if I'm not mistaken."

I was in the Sick Room dormitory with six Orphans, but there was plenty of bare floor between our beds, and Sister Joy kept the windows open. The late summer sun was very hot, and the Sick Room was right under the roof. Tuffy, whose bed was beneath the window, used to flap the curtain to and fro to stir the sultry air. There was a warren of passages up on the top floor, all floored with threadbare brown matting, with rooflights at odd angles, and low white doors leading to queer-shaped empty rooms. Some were used for music practice. Orphans and Providers who wanted a little studio, writing room, or just an empty space, had squatted in hidden places up here. It was much lighter than downstairs, and the crooked angles were somehow welcoming. The lightheaded feeling I'd had when Dennis carried me persisted through my measles: I was too weak to be careful, and that made everything light and easy. Feverish dreams troubled me. It was a relief to wake in the moonlight and see the humped outlines of Jake and Sue in the beds on either side. When we were able to sit up we began to talk a little. Jake knew a lot of jokes, all new and hilarious to me. One day he said, "What did the man say when he came across three holes in the ground?"

"What?"

"Well, well, well."

I was still laughing when Sister Joy came in with our camomile tea. I remember the startled look she gave me, as if I'd been a proper Orphan all the time and she'd never noticed. After the measles Jake chatted to me whenever we met. Sue didn't. The first time I saw her after we were all back at school, she was with her friends and she walked straight past me, pretending not to recognise me. Later she tried to make up for it, but of course I couldn't trust her. Jake remained my friend, but not Sue.

"I hear Basil's leaving us," said Dennis, sipping his tea. "Off to the hills, I gather. Is that what's bothering you?"

"Yes."

"People grow up. Things change. You may want to see the world yourself some day."

"This *is* the world," I said. "It's as much here as anywhere else, isn't it?"

"Yes of course. But that depends on what you think the world is," said Dennis. "We've all come here from somewhere else. Providers, Nunks, Orphans ... we're all in some sort of exile, when you think about it."

"But going away *now* would be just more exile."

"So it would." Talking to Dennis was different from talking to Basil, because Dennis always started by agreeing, more or less, and then making what I said into something different. Basil liked to get straight on with the arguing. Dennis went on, "You can't belong again, once that's gone. I sometimes think about where I came from, but I can't go back. That's exile."

"*Why* can't you go back?"

"It's the other side of the War Zone. At least, it is now. We fled over the mountains when I was a boy, me and my brother, with a group – six, eight, I think we were – mostly men. We were boys; it was all we could do to keep up. Climbing up through the snow in our thin shoes, we just had to stay alive. You're cold. Thirsty, always thirsty. Keep walking. Our family wanted us to go. I remember the crying. You hug someone – last time ever – *ever* – you know it – you walk away. You think, I could run back, just once, hug her again. What would be the point of that? Done now. If you go back just one more time, it's all to do again. It wasn't safe to stay. I don't know if they're still there. I don't know who's alive or who's dead. Sometimes I think, surely they wouldn't hurt them, they weren't doing anyone any harm. Other times I think, no, it doesn't work like that. I won't find out. There's no way back."

"*Basil* thinks he can go back."

"Well, he can make the journey anyway, where he wants to go. It's safe enough these days. I hear there's hardly anyone left up there at all. The drivers say the roads are open now right up to the passes. You have to be careful as you get near the hill country, but people trade all right, and move about. You set off thinking it'll be dangerous, and you'll be scared all the time. Once you're out there, you realise very quickly that most human beings are good. The ones who want to hurt you – they're the ones that make most noise and get heard about. If Basil keeps his ears open and acts accordingly, he'll soon discover that most people are good."

This was a difficult thought, and it took me a while to walk round it. Then I said, "I'm not sure I believe that."

"Worth a journey, maybe, to find out?"

"But Basil doesn't want to find out if most people are *good*." I hated Dennis's habit of changing where we going halfway along. "Basil wants to find out about his *family*."

"Basil wants to grow up," said Dennis. "So his friends have to let him do it."

In the heat of the summer afternoon I laid out racks to dry my herbs. I snipped slowly: feverfew, marjoram, chervil, chicory, oregano. Bees and hoverflies hummed in the lavender. Rock doves murmured from the orchard. Beyond the hedges the woods were in heavy leaf, like a shimmering green sea.

Sea? I was arrested, scissors still, by a clear image inside my head. Not green leaves, blue water, but the shimmering was the same. How did I know that? I had seen the summer trees, as season followed season, more times than I'd bothered to count, but I had never been troubled by any simile before. This was change. I didn't like it. I laid out sprigs of marjoram on the warm rack. While I worked I knew what I was doing. A blue shadow fell across the marjoram. I looked up.

A tall woman stood looking down at me. She had her back to the light, a dark outline. "You're Rue?"

"I'm called Rue, yes." I knew how sulky I sounded, but who'd told her that? Had she asked? Why?

I'd seen her, of course. She was one of the Supplicants, and she came every summer about this time. She used to stroll around the gardens in her long blue tunic. The first time I'd spotted her in the knot garden I'd been watering young parsley in my first quadrangle. I'd frozen, screened from sight – I was much smaller then – behind an ancient rosemary bush. I was fascinated because she moved like a young woman, very straight and tall, but her silver hair flowed down her back, and when I glimpsed her face it was quite old. She wandered round the herb garden as if it were her own. It wasn't, of course, she was just one of the fleeting Supplicants. But she walked as if she *belonged*. As she passed my rosemary bush she pinched a sprig between her fingers, and sniffed the scent of it. Crouching just the other side in the shadows, the thought came clear to me, 'That's how I want to be.' I'd never thought before about what I might become; I'd been too intent on finding safety where I already was.

Every summer she came to the knot garden. The Supplicants wander at will. Sister Angela told me very early on, when I resented their presence, 'The gardens are for the Supplicants. We make them entirely for their solace. When Supplicants wander here, we see our gifts received. That's our privilege. Not everyone gets to see that. You watch, and you'll see.'

I did watch the tall woman with the silver hair. She always walked alone. It was very difficult to regard Supplicants as any kind of privilege when they walked round my paths always talking, not even listening to the garden. When they sat in my place on the sundial steps, sometimes for hours, I spat with fury, but always silently, from a distance. If they saw me, they greeted me casually and moved on. Very occasionally one tried to talk to me, but that never got them anywhere. I regarded the tall woman with silver hair differently. So now, after a moment's hesitation, I stood up.

I was as tall as she was. I hadn't expected that.

"I'm Elena. I've seen you here before, I think. Can we walk around the paths? Sister Angela tells me you look after this garden."

"I look after *half* of it." Then I added, "*Two* quadrangles. This one, with the herbs. And that one, with the flowers." I wasn't sure why I was wasting so many words on a stranger, but she seemed to compel them. I don't know how she made it happen, but as we walked, we talked more about the garden. I answered her questions, and I even found myself telling her things without being asked.

She talked to me about her life. The Supplicants were nothing to do with me, but I found myself listening to her stories.

"I thought it was the most beautiful city in the world," she was saying. "Many people thought that. They came from all over the world to see it. Ruins and rubble now. The gardens are gone, the ancient buildings, the squares with their fountains. The wells, the old walls, the shaded avenues. There are no trees."

"No *trees*?" I was aghast.

"The trees were cut down long ago. Nearly all the people are gone. A few live in shacks among the ruins. We rebuilt a house – not properly, there's no one to do that – but habitable, just about. I look after it. It's called The House for Lost People."

She waited, as if I ought to say something. Unwillingly, because part of me desperately did not want to know, I asked, "Who are the Lost People?"

"I think you know."

I couldn't answer that, and I didn't think she should expect me to.

"It's hard work looking after the House for Lost People. So

once a year I come here as a Supplicant, to be looked after myself. You know that's why so many Supplicants keep coming back? You probably regard us as a nuisance." I could feel her reading my face. "But we all come from somewhere. We all have our reasons. You don't need to hear mine now. I came here with a particular request, and Brother Dennis told me I should speak to you."

"I don't do requests," I told her. "I'm just *here*. I'm not a Nunk or a Provider. Not even an Orphan. *I'm* not the person you want."

"You've just shown me your knot garden. I can see for myself that you are exactly the person I want. I brought another Supplicant with me, but I can't take her away with me."

"*No!* No, I can't ... I'm the wrong person ... You don't ..."

"Don't look so frightened. It's not a person. It's a small dog. I found it in the gutter and I brought it back to the House for Lost People. But our house is for people, not dogs. There are packs of dogs roaming everywhere; people are afraid of them. But this dog is very small. If it were left by itself it would soon die. That's what I should have done: left it in the street to take its chance. There's enough work for us to do. But I was coming here ... it's foolish, but it's very small. I brought it with me. But it can't fit in here either. It's not a useful animal. It's probably an Orphan, but it's not human so it doesn't count. I confessed my foolishness to Brother Anthony, and showed him the little dog. He told me to find Sister Angela, and ask for you."

I didn't protest when Elena took me to the Supplicants' Bookroom and bent over a grubby bag at the fireside. A scrap of dull black fur cowered against stained canvas. Elena scooped her out and passed her to me. I had to hold her. It would have been better to take longer. She was thin as a wisp and trembling all over. Her little heart hammered against my bare arm. Wild-eyed and fearful, she shrunk against me. She thought if she made herself very small I wouldn't notice her enough to hurt her.

I carried her back to the knot garden, murmuring to her as reassuringly as I could. "Do you have a name?" I asked her. "If you already have one you can never tell me." She looked up at me. Her tongue flickered as if she wanted to lick my hand but didn't quite dare. "I shall call you Cosette," I told her.

I called her Cosette because she reminded me of my favourite character in one of the best books we'd read at school. Slowly Cosette got better. Her sores and her limp healed. Her jet black coat grew glossy as I fed her on choice scraps. Her brown eyes brightened, her nose felt damp. She had big ears like a bat and a face like one of the carved devils at the end of the high gutters coming off the Practice Room roof. She was tiny, but her legs were so long for her body she could run like a hare. She was terrified. Any loud noise, any clattering or raised voice, and she'd be there like a streak of lightning, barking furiously. She never attacked, but she annoyed everyone. They said I should smack her, but I knew it was her fear, so I never did. She stayed with me all the time. I kept telling her she was safe. At night she slept with me in my little room, hidden away on one of the crooked corridors beyond the Sick Room, where I'd quietly moved myself in after I'd had the measles.

Cosette liked to doze in the knot garden while I worked. She loved the sun on the warm stone, and used to lie spreadeagled on her back to catch all the heat she could. I built her a little kennel for when it rained. I lined it with rags to be warm in winter. She wasn't allowed in the Refectory so I fed her in her own place by the back door. When I'd finished my work I'd take her into the woods and fields. She loved heading out with me, nose a-quiver and ears pricked. She missed nothing; I only wished she could tell me what she knew. I taught her to avoid the sheep and cattle, and never bark in their presence. It was harder to explain to her that she must never run out and bark at people. Things had once happened – of course she couldn't tell me – which made her too afraid to think sensibly. This habit worried me, because it seemed important that we should be able to stay very quiet and hide ourselves if necessary. Gradually her mind grew still, and she began to listen to me. Sometimes she forgot to obey me when she was frightened. She couldn't help it.

The spring after Basil had left me, and Cosette had come to me, Phyllis came out to the knot garden in her flour-streaked apron as I was sweeping dead leaves off the path. "Rue, the Conductor wants to speak to you." She looked agitated. I'd never been summoned by the Conductor before. I didn't stop to ask why.

I'd heard the grand piano often enough, its notes falling like raindrops from above when the big windows were opened wide. You heard it most clearly in the orchard, but on a still day the faintest of trebles would echo on as far as the knot garden. Sometimes I took my tea and sat right under the window, letting the music flow around me as I gazed unfocused at the apple trees. The Conductor never played at Practice. Sister Ursula sometimes played the piano there at Evening Practice, when the other instruments were absent, but never the Conductor. That music only came to me disembodied. But now, entering the Conductor's Studio for the first time, I saw the grand piano in front of me. I longed to touch those gleaming notes, but I was as likely to lay my fingers on the Moon. With an effort I turned from the music to the Conductor.

"Sit down, Rue."

I sat on the edge of my chair, on the other side of the leather-topped desk.

"You've been with us a long time."

"Yes."

"This is your home."

"Yes."

"No one can stay at home for ever, Rue."

I couldn't say yes to that. I didn't know.

"Rue, when the Orphans grow up, they have to leave us. You know that."

"Yes," I whispered, because my throat was so tight it hurt me.

"Some Orphans come back as Providers. A few – a very few – elect to become Nunks. Sometimes they visit as Supplicants. Many never come back at all. There are some we never hear of again." The Conductor looked out of the window, and added softly, "That always makes me sad."

I couldn't breathe. I knew what was coming.

"Rue, everyone who grows up here must leave. There is a world out there, and you must know it. You can't stay in the knot garden for ever. Once you've set out, you can't turn back. An angel will stand at the gate with a flaming sword, and will not let you pass."

I thought of the knot garden entrances, four arches in the yew hedge – east, north, west, south – all without gates or angels. I must have looked confused.

"Ah yes, your final school report informs me you are a literalist. Let me put it plainly. Rue, it's time for you to leave the garden. You must go into the world, which is where you came from, and find out."

"Find out *what*?"

"Ah yes, you'll need to find the question first. The answer will surely follow."

"But I can come back?"

"That's for you to say. You can't know the answer until you've worked out what the question is. How will you live, do you think?"

I choked back a sob. "I don't know."

"Then think. Sister Angela tells me you're very skilled with herbs. Brother Anselm tells me" – the Conductor glanced down at a paper on the desk – "you 'can play the flute so as to charm the birds off the trees'. Those are skills, Rue. By your skills you can earn your living wherever you go. Think about it, so you can get ready."

I had nothing to say. I got up to go.

"Rue!"

"Yes?"

"If you try to come back too soon, the angel with the sword will be at the gate. Only you will know when the path is open. This is your home, and when – if – the time comes we'll kill the fatted calf for you. But not before."

"Fatted calf?" I was utterly bewildered now, and much too frightened to work it out. Besides, I never ate meat. Perhaps the Conductor didn't know that.

"We all wish you well, Rue. You gave us more than you know. Fare well."

Three
Maze

The magician said, "This is the card – here. Look at it, and tell me what you see."

I took the card gingerly. The Nunks taught us to beware of any gift which seems uncanny, because it's almost certainly a lie, and lies are dangerous. The uncanny is not in anyone else's gift; you can only find it on your own. But when I looked at the picture, my first thought was that it was innocent. It was a picture of innocence anyway; I wasn't sure that was the same thing.

It showed a young man in motley walking along a road. Not so much walking as dancing. He had a knapsack on his back and an oxeye daisy in his left hand. Running beside him was a small black dog, so like Cosette that I gasped. There she was, with her long legs and thin wavy tail, her bat ears and clever pointy face. The sky was blue; a butterfly fluttered by. But there were cruel snow-capped peaks in the distance, and – I gasped again, in fear more than surprise this time – right in front of the young man's heedless feet a chasm split the earth. And Cosette was looking at him, her eyes filled with trust. He was going to let her fall in. He was going to fall in himself, come to that, but he should have known better.

"Do you recognise it?"

"I recognise Cosette," I admitted unwillingly.

"Do you not see yourself?"

"*Myself?*" I bent over the card again and studied it minutely. At last I answered, "I see the part I play."

"A wise answer. Do you know who he is?"

"You just said he was *me*."

"He's the Joker. He has no suit. No number. The Joker in the pack."

"I *never* joke." I wondered if that were true, and added, "I have a friend who makes jokes, but I don't think *I* can."

The only uncanny thing the magician actually did was to produce a rabbit out of his hat. We saw it when we joined the audience by the broken market cross, where some of the houses round the square had been repaired to form an enclosed yard. Cosette sat on my knee, back straight, ears cocked, watching attentively. All the magician's other tricks had a logical explanation, but I've puzzled over that rabbit ever since. It was a longhaired white rabbit with blue eyes, and although it appeared and disappeared several times it didn't seem to mind at all. I suppose it knew where it was all the time. The next day Cosette and I moved on, and we never saw the magician again. He must have taken the other road.

The Conductor hadn't known as much about the ways of the world as I'd thought. Only once did someone give me food in exchange for hearing me play the flute, and that was a blind madwoman alone on a ruined farm, and she talked no sense anyway. Her food was very dirty, but I was so hungry I didn't care. No one wanted my herbs either. They didn't know who I was, so why should they trust me? Luckily it was lambing time, and I soon found work. Cosette and I hated approaching strange doors but we had to do it. Every farm and hamlet had its guard dogs, so we always had to arrive openly by the main track. As soon as the dogs got wind of us the barking would start. I taught Cosette to leap into my arms and be silent, which was more dangerous for me, but Cosette's trouble was that she'd survived up until now by pretending to attack first, and she never seemed to realise how small she was.

We knew that once the people had accepted us we'd have no more trouble with the dogs. We also learned fast that everyone wanted us – at least, they wanted the work I could do, and were prepared to feed both of us. Cosette did her part by playing with the children. She somehow knew about children, and wagged her lanky tail – unusual for her, in the early days – whenever she saw any. It was our advantage that there was no labour to be had. Even though people usually said, "You're a bit skinny. We'll see if you're strong enough for the work," they always wanted me to stay after a day's trial. Sometimes they tried to persuade us to stay longer, saying there were other jobs to be done. But Cosette and I were on a journey. Although we had no idea where we were going, it was important not to get sidetracked.

Wherever we walked, we found fields untilled, pastures overgrown and the wild remnants of herds and flocks. Cosette hated the dogs howling at night. It wasn't the animals I minded, but wherever we found traces of feral people we went another way. Cosette and I each feared our own kind more than anything else in the world. On the other hand, we liked the way the forest was reclaiming its own – an unstoppable advance of green which hurt no one and engulfed everything – "faster than a thought" one farmer told me.

We found a city clothed in green. Groping roots were pulling apart houses, squares, streets, shops and warehouses. Had it happened faster the noise must have been tremendous, but as it was, to our quick ears there was only a consuming silence. Everywhere the stinging nettles were almost as tall as I was; I could see where Cosette was going because they shook as she pushed her way through. We followed bramble-choked streets bright with daisies, campion, foxgloves, angelica and willow herb. Young birches burst through broken roofs. We crossed jagged thresholds into crazy rooms, all leading into one another but open to the sky. Creeper-covered gaps had once been windows, through which chequered sunlight flickered on the smashed-up tiles. We daren't go under the drooping roofs, but we peered into the darkness. Once we disturbed a sow with piglets. Sparrows rose from the ivy and rabbits scuttled out of dandelion-yellow courtyards when they heard our footsteps. A roe deer bounded from a doorway, and I hissed at Cosette not to chase it. I was afraid she'd get lost in these labyrinthine alleys. In one place we found an adder curled up on a broken flagstone, and in the room beyond there was a table spread with ghostly cups and plates. One day the Refectory might look like that. I called Cosette to come away, and soon after we left the city.

Everywhere we stayed, once folk were gathered round the fire in the evenings, the stories began: "I remember …" "I remember …" Cosette and I usually went to our lair earlier than anyone else. I found the enigma of the magician's white rabbit more enticing than other people's unhappiness.

I earned our keep, and a little more, through strawberry time and haytime, through picking raspberries, blackcurrants, figs, apricots, mulberries, grapes and apples. Potato fields: endless grubbing in warm earth in summer, freezing in winter. Then corn. I'd learned long ago to reap and bind. All the Orphans have to help with that. Midwinter I worked in frozen fields of kale, cabbages and leeks – Cosette hated the icy mornings, but I wrapped her in her blanket, and at least her paws were never frozen to the bone like mine. The work was hard, but there was always plenty of it.

Then came the hungry gap, and for a while that was bad. Cosette and I kept walking under wintry skies, through empty villages and graveyards, past derelict fields along vanishing paths. Cosette would sometimes disappear into the undergrowth and come back with a whitened bone. Once she beat off a bevy of kites and snatched half a rabbit. I was terrified a kite would carry her off. Cosette wasn't scared. She thought she was a wolf, and she wasn't far wrong, except about her size, of which she hadn't a notion. Not being a scavenger, I fared worse, until at last, one icy morning under a cold sun, we came over a pass and looked down on the sea.

The sea sparkled too bright to bear, yet I couldn't look away. My eyes hurt; water ran down my cheeks. The sea shimmered, just like … like … I thought of the summer trees shimmering in the haze beyond the knot garden. I conjured up the knot garden itself, its four quadrangles, its enclosing paths, the angles of the box hedges, the sundial in the middle, the curve of warm steps. Gradually the world reconfigured. I breathed again, and looked it in the face. The sea was a shining emptiness stretching to an inconceivable horizon. I sniffed, and before I even caught the tang of salt, I knew exactly what the smell would be.

Inside my mind appeared a wooden shed. A wide door, open to a shingle beach. A honey-coloured boat, upside down on trestles. Smell of salt water mingled with fresh-sawn shavings. Tools, back there in the gentle dark, tools handled with skill and knowledge. Seamed hands … Hands …

Cosette licked my hand: come on, it's all right, we'd better get going. She trotted along neatly, tail curled jauntily over her back, legs going like a kestrel's wings. I fell into pace behind her as I always did, heading downhill towards that disquieting sea.

Most people don't want to hurt you. If they're afraid they'll attack, but hardly anyone felt threatened by us. Cosette would tell me at once if anyone was dangerous, and I'd taught her how to melt into the shadows and not be noticed. The more people there are, the safer it is. The best place to hide a book is in a library; all you have to do is put it where it doesn't belong. The trick is not to let them place you. Cosette and I grew very good at that.

So when we reached the city, on the southern shore of a wide estuary, we didn't hesitate. No one knew we were together; that was our way of making ourselves invisible. Cosette trotted a few paces ahead, ears back, tail low, weaving her way out of reach of any passer by. She looked back at every turning for me to covertly point out the way. The streets were full of soldiers. We knew better than to slink away; we strolled among the people as if we walked there every day. I kept my eyes away from the soldiers, and Cosette took no notice at all. I wondered if she'd ever seen guns before. We threaded our way through a maze of narrow streets, always heading downhill, until we reached the harbour. The sea wall had been breached by bomb craters, and the main jetties were in ruins, but there was a rutted slipway where small boats were moored. A bigger ship rode at anchor in the bay. The sight of it brought my heart to my mouth. Without stopping to ask why I turned to flee. Cosette ignored me. Nose twitching, she made a dash for a pile of fish boxes at the top of the jetty. The man unloading them aimed a kick. Cosette broke into shrill barking and bared her teeth. I rushed to grab her. Now we were right out in the open on the bare quay. Strangers were looking at us. I didn't dare run. I held Cosette tightly and walked away. I could feel the crowd's eyes on my shrinking back, but I made myself walk slowly.

Once out of sight, we followed a rutted path, with warehouses on the seaward side, and inhabited houses on our right. In front of us small waves lapped at a black sandy beach. On the other side of the street there was an open shop front.

That is how I found Luisa. The herbs drew my attention first. I breathed in the familiar scent, and my heart relaxed. Bunches of thyme, mint, sage and lavender hung from the eaves of the open shop. They drew me in. There were the herbs, a tapestry of greens varying from grey to blue to yellowish, neatly fitted into a carved tray of square wooden boxes. Dried herbs like the dark better; someone must cover them when selling time was over because their colours were still good. But as nothing – I stood agape – their colours were as nothing compared to the others. Yellow, orange, ochre, brown, reds of every shade, fine as sand or large as hazelnuts, all the colours of the earth distilled into little boxes with an intensity I had never seen before. They smelt of heat and far-off places. I thought of the globe in the Orphans' classroom. I'd always loved to turn it, learning by heart the patterns of blue and green and brown, the shapes of continents and seas. Our globe had relief carved on it, so you could run your forefinger across the world and touch the highest peaks and deepest troughs, and feel the actual outlines of the islands.

I was still standing there when Luisa came out. "You're interested in our spices?"

"What are their names?" I was too absorbed to glance at her, and I'd forgotten all about the pleasantries with which Phyllis had taught me to start a conversation. "Where do they come from?"

Our partnership began as a litany: caraway, cardamom, cloves, cumin, cayenne, cinnamon, saffron … turmeric, ginger, nutmeg, peppercorns. Countries I'd thought were lost for ever, green oases where we'd learned there was nothing left but desert, lava islands where we'd been told that ships no longer sailed. There was still living land out there, and people who belonged there.

"… only very recently," Luisa told me later. "Very little, very expensive, but a few years ago the first spice ship came. They'd had a rough voyage, stormy and often out of sight of land. Very dangerous. My mother … people told them who we were – who my family had once been – so they came here. The man came to our door and said, 'They say you were once spice merchants in this city.' When they showed us their samples – they had them in little canvas bags – I'd never seen such colours before – such wonderful scents – my mother – *my mother* – broke down and wept. I'd never seen that before, not in all those years. Not when they … I was the one left. I was the baby, asleep upstairs. They shot my father dead. They raped my mother and took the children. They never found me. The city was burnt, everything. Of course when we came back, years later, I couldn't remember. I grew up in the rubble. It was different for her. She was a hard woman. She couldn't forgive me for not being … for not remembering … She kept me alive. I have to remember that. But when the ship came, and they showed us the spices – that was when she wept. After all those years. I understand it better now. She hated the soldiers always being here. Couldn't get used to it. In the end she just never went out."

Cosette quickly made herself at home in the house behind the shop. As the sun moved round she'd drag her bed into each new patch of sunlight on the kitchen floor, arrange it to her liking, and settle into it. She liked to be in the middle of the room so she could keep an eye on all three doors. Luisa soon learned not to trip over her. Cosette preferred the doors open; Luisa liked them shut. I taught Cosette not to bark at customers, and that she had to do what Luisa told her even if she didn't like it. Even if I wasn't there. After that we all got on well. In the evenings they both liked to listen when I played my flute.

Fetching water and foraging for firewood took a long time every day. Luisa kept two chickens in the yard, and she grew herbs in pots on the rooftop. Everything else had to be bought each day in the market. Even bread. There were shortages and long queues. I didn't take Cosette; she hated standing in the rain all day. I'd had no notion how much time most people spend keeping themselves alive. In winter it seemed worth the effort. It was warm by the kitchen fire, and the stone walls held us safely. Luisa used a word that was new to me: 'cosy'. For her, 'cosy' was the ultimate goal. Cosette loved 'cosy' too. For Cosette it was after supper when humans sit down. She would leap on to my knee and arrange herself in comfort, making small protesting yowls if I dared move, or, worse still, stand up. Only when winter came did I define 'cosy' for myself. It meant not being out in an icy field cutting off frozen cabbage heads with numb fingers.

Once the blackthorn was out I grew impatient with 'cosy'. There was still a world out there, and Cosette and I were on a journey. It was Luisa's idea that I should take to the road with our herbs and spices. She said she couldn't stand me prowling;

there wasn't room. Cosette and I very quickly found that peddling was a better way to live, if you had high-class wares like ours which didn't weigh too much. Our sales brought us food and shelter, and coins as well. When I carried too many coins for comfort, and my stocks were running low, I went back to Luisa, and then when I was ready I set off again. I acquired regular customers. Even their dogs were always glad to see us. Some customers liked me to play my flute in the evenings. As the seasons passed I found other spice merchants in other places, and I was able to replenish my stock without going home. These people had ways of carrying money, so I could send coins back to Luisa without having to go all the way myself. A merchant – I got to know him well – told me that the coins Luisa received might not be exactly the same ones I'd handed over, but he'd make sure they were worth the same. I knew I could trust him, and so it proved. Cosette and I felt free to explore new country. When the days grew shorter we turned for home. Cosette made it very clear that in winter she preferred to be cosy.

Many seasons passed. Cosette acquired a little line of grey hair under her chin. She was seldom freakish now, but always ready for the road. She still trotted ahead, tail curled like a banner, eyes alert, nose twitching, the most familiar sight in my world. Each summer we went a little further, and found new customers and new views into unknown country.

We came to the foothills where fighting had been recent. The slopes were scarred by explosions, not yet greened over. Ruined villages held signs of recent life. We found a house where tatters of washing still hung on the line. We peered into a dark doorway and heard rats scuttling. We turned a corner. The remains of a human body – a man – I saw it all in a moment and wished I had not – lay rotting in the yard.

Cosette nudged my leg. She was trembling. "We're going back," I told her, and we slunk away.

We came to thick forest criss-crossed by a maze of grass-grown tracks. When Cosette heard anyone coming, which was seldom, we hid in the undergrowth until they'd passed. In the depths of the trees, with a strip of cloudy sky overhead, I was beginning to lose direction as well as trust. "Cosette, are you quite sure of the way back?" Of course she was, but she didn't understand what I was asking.

By the time we came to the abandoned city on the headland we were very hungry. We approached warily. No dogs barked and I wondered if this place too were deserted. Then I saw smoke rising from a chimney. The city was enclosed by an ancient wall, mellow with age and covered with little ferns and ground ivy, green and pink. The afternoon sun against that warm wall seemed very old and very new at the same time. It felt familiar, yet all this place was strange to me. I followed a beaten track along the side of the wall. We came to a high archway. There were rusted hinges on one side where a great gate once hung. For once I led, and Cosette followed at my heels. She seemed to think I knew where I was.

The streets were overgrown and almost empty. The house with the smoking chimney had a couple of tables outside. A few people were eating and drinking silently. I thought of the Providers' laden tables in the orchard, the sound of laughter and the noisy chat which used to hurt my ears. I'd have given anything to hear it now.

"A *spice* merchant? However did you get here?"

"I came through the forest."

"Just you, and your little dog? I don't believe it. You must have a charmed life! Who are you? Where are you from?"

"They call me Rue."

"You'd do better to go back by the coast, Rue."

"Is there a road?"

"You'd be safer going by boat. Now, we want to see your wares."

"Can I have something to eat first?"

They had bread, and good cheese; they must have kept flocks near by. They didn't look hungry, but I could feel the unhappiness in the air. There weren't many of them and they were all old. They recognised my herbs and most of the spices. One exclaimed in delight, "I never thought to see such again! But are they expensive? Do you want money for them?"

"I can give you some for no money if you let me rest here a day or two, and give us food. Where are we? What is this place?"

They glanced at one another and no one seemed to want to answer. Finally an old, gnarled woman looked at me sadly and said, "This is no longer a place. It used to be a fine city, but the people … some fought back … We're no longer on the map. No one was left. Just a few of us came down from the hills and stayed. *They* didn't bother to come back. We've not been disturbed since."

They made much of Cosette and me, but we longed to get away. They said they'd tell me when there was a boat, but no one could tell me how long that would be. They were vehemently against us taking the coast road, and I didn't want to face the desolation of the hills again.

A steep paved road, covered with heaps of rubble and interspersed with flights of broken steps, led to the top of the town. There had been a courtyard here. A spreading cedar tree, untouched, shaded the parapet. I pressed the soft bark of the cedar with my fingers as if it were a forgotten friend, and stared out to sea. The waves were white-capped. Grey clouds scudded overhead. The wind whipped my hair across my face. There'd be no boat today. The thought came into my head as if someone had spoken it, with authority. And yet I knew nothing about boats.

Facing the sea across the square, still intact, was the facade of a noble building. It reminded me of the Practice Room. And of something else, dragging at me like a little clenched-toothed dog. Cosette whined: let's go away. I turned back to follow her. My mouth felt suddenly dry. But the place was deserted. Cosette would have told me if it wasn't. I had to look. The iron-studded doors were twice as tall as I was, but one was wedged a little open. I swallowed, went up three shallow marble steps, and peeped inside.

There was no roof. I could see the mosaics on the wall. The mosaics on the ... The mosaics ... The golden dragon ... the horse ... the charging spear. The mosaics ...

The past crashed down

shouting pushing shots shots shots running into each other shots never stopping screaming smell of fear shots smoke choking screaming screaming screaming silence. Someone groaning. Silence. Silence. I could not move.

Blood, sticky where I knelt. My eyes uncovering. Bodies. Dead.

Heaped up. Dead people. Strange angles. Blood. Silence. Blood. My people. Silent. Standing up, shaking, shaking, shaking, so slow, so slow, not being able to breathe.

She lay splayed beside me. Blood on my knees, my hands, my shirt. Her blood.

running running running down the street down the steps away away away just like before

there was a boat I did not care how dangerous it was

waves breaking over us the boat full of water they were strangers far too many

we did not die

she said don't speak don't say a word don't tell anyone what you are they will kill you so you must never, ever, say your name

I was so small they didn't see me

I was the only one but I cannot speak they will kill me

I did not die

A unicursal maze is one that leads unerringly through many convolutions to its central point. There are no divergences. You don't have to solve it; you just have to trust it. Your intuition may cry out against it, but, unlike a puzzle maze, it won't deceive you. Many people believe they make their own decisions. A few lay down their lives for the right to think this. I would not. After much thought, much reading, and many conversations, mostly with myself, I decided the unicursal maze was the correct choice for the third quadrangle.

I started working on the design long before I reached home. The first person I discussed it with was Luisa. She said, "Yes, I can see you need to do this. You must go. I don't have to understand."

"There's nothing to understand. I just want it to be the right *pattern*."

"Most people would be asking questions."

"How do you *mean*?"

"Well, that's a question, I suppose. So is 'Why?' a question. Or 'Who?' Or 'How?' Or 'Who are we?' Or 'What happened?'"

"I don't understand."

"I know you don't. You go off and make your unicursal maze." She seemed about to say something else, but then she turned away. I bent over my drawing again.

My final design eventually covered the whole window table in the Nunks' library. I went back to it every evening after it was too dark to work outside. Cosette lay on the hearthrug where I had lain long ago, soaking up the heat. Sometimes a Nunk would come to look over my shoulder. Brother Simon, who'd taught me geometry in school, showed me how to use his protractor and compasses so I could make circles inside squares, and triangles in the resulting corners with one curved side.

Before the spring equinox I had my third quadrangle laid out with pegs and string. I laid out the box hedges under a waxing moon. Sister Angela watched from her wheeled chair, critical as ever, but she couldn't hide her delight. I'd come home to find the whole knot garden waist high in dockens, nettles, ground elder and rose bay willow herb. All my precious herbs were left untended, except for a plot of common kitchen herbs which Dennis kept in order for the Providers. The box hedges had spread across the paths and some of my rarest specimens had disappeared completely. I spent the autumn nursing my two quadrangles back to health before I could even begin to till the third for planting. Then I marked out my maze and planted out the little sprigs of box. As the days lengthened I built paths of flagstones interspersed with cobbles in flowing patterns. When I got nearer the centre, Cosette abandoned her favourite spot on the sundial steps, and dragged her bed to the empty space in the middle of the maze. I knelt on the path, trowel in hand, bucket of mortar at my side, laying my cobblestones. As I slowly drew closer to the centre, I began to think about what should be there.

Autumn was turning into winter when I went to see Ellen, who used to teach us art. She had a studio in one of the old stables. I walked in without knocking, just as I used to do as a child. "I need a mosaic."

"Ah Rue, it's you! I'm so glad you've come back. I've seen your wonderful maze. Are you still working on it? Is the mosaic to be part of it?"

"Yes. I need you to tell me how to make it."

The mosaic was the hardest part to do. Many seasons passed before I was satisfied with it. Spring came round again, and then again. I was working in the knot garden every day, just as I used to do, and also helping the Providers with all the jobs I'd learned when I was on the road. I milked goats, helped with lambing, picked fruit and harvested crops. One or two of the Providers became my friends. I always refused to help in the school, and I avoided the new Orphans as much as I could. They were all much younger than me now. Most of them came from the House for Lost People. There weren't enough War

Orphans any more, so the rules had been changed while I was away. The mosaic took shape, and slowly turned from grey paper plans to brightly-coloured stone. A scarlet and gold dragon curled around the epicentre of my maze. His tongue was crimson, his flames orange and yellow and red. His claws were tipped with silver, his scales curled and shone. He was quite alone. No one was coming to kill *him*.

My dragon had nowhere to land. Very tentatively, I began to sketch him a background. I went back to Ellen and she ordered the tiles I wanted. It was a while before I was ready to lay them down, but as soon as I did I could see the dragon had found his place. It fitted him exactly. All around the epicentre I laid down a mosaic of blues and greens and greys, a sea of shifting colours, white-edged waves. Sometimes I stopped and screwed up my eyes, remembering the sea in my mind, trying to bring it into focus. Too often it slid away from me; I couldn't keep it still. Things were shifting around inside my head, and the mosaic often made patterns I hadn't yet dreamed of, but the colours told my fingers what to do. All I had to do was follow.

Cosette wanted no more adventures. She was happy with the maze. The box hedges were thick and bushy now, taller than she was. She liked trotting up and down the cobbled paths, to the centre and back again. She never jumped over the hedges; she knew things didn't work like that. She basked in the sun on the sundial steps, or in her chosen place at the centre of the maze. When I worked in the fields or orchards I took her cushion so she could settle near me and doze the day away. In wet weather I'd leave her by the fire in the library; she always knew I'd soon be back. She loved the drying room, where I hung the herbs, and then prepared and stored them. She liked the mixture of smells in there. She couldn't walk far now, so I carried her in my knapsack, her head peeping out at the top. In the evenings, when we settled by the fire in the Providers' sitting room or the Nunks' Library, Cosette no longer leaped on to my knee, but waited patiently for me to lift her up. Her eyebrows and muzzle were white, her glossy black fur flecked with grey, but her eyes were as bright as ever, her bat ears still cocked for every passing sound. Her oldness broke my heart, because I was still quite young, but at least I knew I'd always be able to look after her.

It wasn't long after the sea mosaic was finished that I lost my sweet Cosette. She died in her sleep on her cushion on the sundial steps, on a summer afternoon when the birds were silent in the heat and the bees buzzed among the box and lavender. I made Cosette's grave at the heart of my maze, in the empty space which I'd never worked out how to fill. I put a river-rounded sandstone block over it, and on it I carved her name: 'Cosette'. I'm no stone carver, but I did the best I could.

Something was still missing. All winter it nagged at me. I walked round and round my maze in rain and fog and snow, among my box hedges all bravely weathering the winter. I had no small shadow at my heels now, no neat little figure trotting ahead, long black tail curled merrily over her back. I stared down at the frosty dragon and the dragon looked sideways at me. I looked into the depths of the sea. It seemed so real its salt spray stung my eyelids. Blues and greens and greys mingled and shifted in water-filtered light. Salt water ran down my cheeks. It dripped off my chin as I gazed at Cosette's name carved, not very well, on the honey-coloured stone. A heavy stone inside me pressed against my heart. I hadn't known it was there, but now it was swelling up, exploding inside my chest and choking me. I forgot to be insignificant. I only remembered that I – *I* – had been somewhere all the time even when I was invisible. I flung myself down on Cosette's stone and sobbed so hard the sparrows flew away, and even the doves rose from the yews protesting.

Before spring came I added two more words to my carving. Just under where it said 'Cosette' I carved, a bit crookedly, in spite of all my careful measurements, 'And Others'. And so at last the third quadrangle was done.

Four

Solace

I reached the House for Lost People by a convoluted route. I lived wild, avoiding contact with my kind. It was better to be cold. I found a hollow tree and for a while I lived there. I made my bed with dried moss and heather stalks, but whenever I grew warm I couldn't bear it. On icy nights I threw off my layers and flung myself face down under the stars, pressed against the frozen ground. I was so cold that everything became very clear. I lay on the ground and saw in front of my eyes dead leaves, stones, acorn cups, beech mast, knotted roots. They took on a sharpness that made me catch my breath. The brown leaves under my hands were soft as feathers. The vibrancy of dormant life, waiting, things you never see when you are warm. The edge of life is so sharp it hurts, but that was easier than the melting. The less I had to eat, the brighter the edges grew. I felt more alive that way. I didn't care if the cold killed me. I don't know why it didn't, except that more of life still waited, but I didn't know that yet.

I walked barefoot in the snow, and my feet felt the pain as none of the rest of me did. They refused to go on. My sore feet drove me back to my bed in the hollow tree and made me rub them warm and put my socks back on. My feet brought me back from the edge and insisted on being comforted.

I followed the otters' path and saw where they fished, and I fished there too. The squirrels had left some acorns. The acorns were bitter and made me sick; I had no way to prepare them. I watched the squirrels and saw where they dug. I found their store of hazelnuts, and I took more than half, which I knew was too much, but I was very hungry. So I had to leave my hollow tree. I walked downriver until I reached farmland. I stole potatoes from the ground, and turnips left for the cattle. I grew bolder, and took kale from a garden, just a leaf from every plant. I watched the milch cows for a long time. I singled out one and fed her chicory from my hand until she let me milk her a little into my cup. Her milk was thick and warm. But I couldn't make fire unseen so close to the farm, so I went upriver again, with a cheese and a loaf of bread I'd taken through the larder window. They'd notice that. I knew I couldn't go there again. I found winter cress and half-rotten crab apples to eat along with the cheese. The days grew longer, and one afternoon I felt the first heat from the young sun and realised I was starved with cold. I felt dizzy when I stood up. I had forgotten I was hungry. My clothes were torn and filthy, my boots leaked on wet ground. I went back to the human road and started walking.

I was too weak to work, and I couldn't beg. I stole my way to the city far inland. I didn't let anyone see me until I reached it. Then I asked the way to the House for Lost People. When I got there I didn't dare knock at the door. Instead I sank down on the worn doorstep. The closed door was warm against my back. I think I fell asleep.

I was ill in the House for Lost People. There was a roof-light just above me and I lay looking at the sky. The clouds changed hour by hour, sometimes slowly and sometimes scudding fast. Sometimes they were white as lambs against blue sky, sometimes they piled up in stormy towers. Often they were low and grey. I watched them until the daylight faded. On cold nights I saw the stars. Before long I realised there were many other people in the room, the mattresses crowded together so close we were almost touching. It was better to watch the clouds. My bed was soft, with a thick down cover. I had a cup of cool water at my side. When I shivered with cold someone wrapped a hot brick in a towel and laid it at my feet. More hot food appeared than I could eat. I was safe and warm; I never wanted to move again. But then someone brought me clean clothes, and as soon as I was able to go down the staircases I found a way outside. There was a little yard at the back, with a few bedraggled plants in pots and a rough bench by the door. Every fine day the sun lingered on the bench for a little longer.

Elena came. "They told me I'd find you here. You're looking much better, Rue. How are you feeling?"

"I don't know."

"Well, ask yourself. How do you feel?"

I looked at my hands. Empty, they felt nothing. It was an impossible question.

"Rue, I went on a Supplicants' pilgrimage in the autumn, the first I'd managed for years. They told me you'd left without telling anyone, on a night of wind and rain when no one would have set foot outside if they didn't have to. You'd just vanished, like a thief in the night. Your friends were upset. Alarmed about you. And hurt too. Why did you do that?"

"I don't know." I was still staring at my hands. They used to be rough from working. They didn't seem to belong to me any more.

"I saw how your maze had grown since I last saw it, and I looked at your beautiful mosaic. You were making a wonderful garden, Rue." Elena paused. "They told me your little dog had died."

My hands were smooth and empty. They had not touched anything alive for a long time.

"I am so glad I found her," said Elena. "She had a very happy life with you."

I looked at her as if she were the first person I'd seen in my life. "I want to see where you found Cosette."

I, who had crossed hills and deserts, plains, forests, fens, rivers and seas, and reached faraway cities, was exhausted by the time we'd walked a little way uphill. We came to a dirty alley with steps leading up to the main square. High above us sunshine gleamed on wet rooftops, but down here it was dank and smelt of sewage.

Elena stopped. "She was in the gutter. Just here. I wouldn't have seen her, she was so black. But I caught a tiny movement out of the corner of my eye. When I looked down, I saw her eyes gleaming. She was watching me. As if she were waiting. I couldn't pass by. Not when she'd seen me see her."

I stood very still, and thought about Cosette: how frail she'd been when she arrived, how rough her fur was, how she'd limped on her spindly legs. And how frightened she was. It had taken me years to teach her not to be frightened.

"It was pitiful," said Elena. "It was mad to pick her up – I had no idea what I could do with her."

"Pitiful." I repeated. "Do you mean her, or you?"

Elena looked at me curiously. "I mean I felt pity for her. You must know what that means."

"Pity is the pain you feel when something else is suffering?"

"Not at all. Pity is feeling the pain of someone else's suffering." Elena kept on studying me, and as I still said nothing, she added, "Rue, you can stay at the House for Lost People until you're ready to go back to your knot garden." She held up her hand to stop me answering. "Oh yes, you will go back. Your work there isn't finished. Meanwhile you can stay with us. You're well enough to work now, and there's a lot to do."

"I can't work indoors."

"I know. You can work in the yard."

"There's nothing in the yard but a pot of mint. And thyme. And lemon balm. Your parsley's dead. No one's watered it. That isn't enough for me to do."

"Yes it is. I want you to work in the yard. Some of the Lost People like to sit there sometimes. Make them welcome if they do. I'm sure you made people welcome in your knot garden."

I frowned. "I never took any notice of them. I just let them sit there."

"Perfect. You can start tomorrow."

Finding soil was the first problem. Luckily I was a patient thief. I went out very early in the mornings and filled my bag with soil from well-fed gardens. The bag was small enough to hide in my knapsack. No one would miss that much soil. Every day I brought back enough to fill one big pot. I soon ran out of pots. I found middens nearby, and dug into them. There were containers of all kinds: cracked crockery, tins, jars, broken boxes, even old boots. Anything that could still hold soil I brought back to the yard. I took slips where herbs flourished in ruined streets and broken buildings. I stole welsh onions, chives and parsley from backyards. I collected nasturtiums, marigold and forget-me-not seedlings from garden plots. There were too many for anyone to miss them. For water I used the pump outside the kitchen.

I got used to people sitting on the bench watching me. One

day I was sowing sunflower seeds. I'd pinched them from a jar in the kitchen, which is why I jumped when a voice right at my shoulder said, "Can I do some?"

It was a small boy. I thought about how to get rid of him. "You'll have to do it yourself. This box is mine."

He seized a broken cup, and rammed soil into it from the bag. "Give me a seed."

"You have to wet the soil first." I watched critically, and when he'd done it right I handed him a seed. I hesitated and gave him another. "Put in two. One is sure to grow."

After a while I got used to having him around. "My name is Kim," he told me. He got quite good at watering. One day he brought another child. "She wants to plant some too."

I had to dig deep into the midden to find more pots. Soon there was a row of pots all along the sunny side of the yard. I let them scratch their names on the pots so each child knew which was theirs. The seedlings started to sprout. I found an old washtub with no bottom, filled it with soil, and let them sow snapdragons, pansies and mignonette. When Elena came to see me I was grumbling. "I can't give seeds to every single snotty child that comes in here."

"Why not?" she asked, which was less than helpful.

I was running out of space. The next thing I knew, she'd sent one of the old men along with some bits of salvaged wood and some nails. He made more shelves for the pots. He had only one eye, so he always seemed to be measuring his work sideways. At first I was terrified because he wore a ragged soldier's jacket as if he felt at home in it, but it turned out he was just another of the Lost People. By this time there were over twenty sunflowers, each one more than a foot high. Uninvited, the man came back with a friend, a burly man with tattooed arms who wore an empty gunbelt round his waist. They were each carrying a tottering pile of real, whole, terracotta flowerpots. "Where did you find those?" I asked, startled out of my silence.

The old man laid his finger along the side of his nose and winked at his friend. The friend came back next day with a tray of pelargoniums, red and orange and pink. It seemed better not to ask. I let the children plant them. Next thing I knew, someone brought in a table, and soon there were improvised benches round it. I could hardly move to get any work done. The yard was tiny, and when the benches were full the Lost People would talk until my head ached. There was one old woman called Dorothy who always brought her knitting. She sat on her particular stool in the sunniest place by the door, next to a pot of sweet peas, and clicked away with her needles as if she owned the place. For some reason people always wanted to talk to her, and soon there was another stool for the talking person to sit on. Sometimes they sat there until far into the night. I got no peace. It was chaos. All I could think of now was how soon I could get out of here.

Elena said, "You've done a wonderful job, Rue."

I scowled.

"You've made a lot of people feel better. Aren't you pleased?"

"Why should I be?" I felt as surly as I sounded. "They're not my people."

"This is the House for Lost People, Rue, and you live in it. Don't you care what happens to them?"

That was the very question Luisa always used to ask me. I looked away. "No. Why should I?"

"You couldn't have made this garden if you were really as ruthless as that."

I jumped, as if she'd touched my heart with an ice-cold knife.

Elena was watching me; she never missed a thing. "If you were truly ruthless, you wouldn't have looked after the little dog."

I was never ruthless. The next day, Poor Jo came into the yard and lay down by Dorothy's empty stool. I called him Poor Jo because he reminded me of someone in a book we'd read at school, the only character, in fact, that I remembered from the story. I soon stopped calling him Poor, and he just became Jo. When he arrived his reddish coat was matted and mangy. One of his ears was missing. He was so thin I could feel all his ribs and his knobbly backbone. Under his fur he was just a skeleton. His eyes were dull, his nose dry. I fed him on kitchen scraps until his ribs were well covered. His coat grew smooth and glossy. I let him shelter under the table when it rained. After a while I gave him a scrap of blanket to lie on. He was nothing to look at, just an ugly half-grown mongrel like so many others that scavenged the city. I said to him sometimes, "It's no use looking at me like that. I've no room left in my heart for you." He didn't understand, or chose not to.

When I set off home, Jo came with me. He never trotted ahead, but always followed me, his nose almost touching my ankle. When things were good he carried his bushy tail like a tattered banner. When the way got tough his tail went down and his crooked ear went back, but he never complained. He never spoke to anyone unless I did. He was my shadow.

Jo settled down in the knot garden as if he'd been born there. I was relieved he didn't need attention because there was so much to do. I replaced many of the shrubs I'd planted long ago in the first quadrangle. They'd grown battered and leggy, dead in the middle. I trimmed back the bay tree, and set new cuttings from the old rosemaries, sages and lavenders. I divided carpets of mint and borage, and sowed fresh parsley and chervil. I took a risk and for the first time I sowed basil and coriander in the garden itself. I protected them on all sides with slates, and a sheet of glass over the top at night. I weeded out endless fennel shoots, which no other plant likes near them. I cut back the thyme hard, and made a pattern with the subtle shades of new varieties.

The marigolds in the second quadrangle had gone crazy, obliterating anything more tentative. I gradually made the beds over to fragrant flowers in softer colours: wallflowers, pinks, sweet williams, columbines and night-scented stocks. On summer evenings the sumptuous scents permeated the whole knot garden. I put honeysuckle, lilac and hollyhocks against the house wall beyond. Not that summer, but the one after, one of the Supplicants brought an old English shrub rose, bare rooted. I'm surprised it survived the journey; she'd let it dry right out. I had to revive it with a lot of water and attention. I took out the old lavender, which was all woody by now anyway, and planted the rose at the centre of the second quadrangle. It turned out to have small sweet-smelling single flowers, and better still, it kept on flowering right into the autumn. Now it's a great bushy mound which completely covers the round bed in the centre.

The maze in the third quadrangle only needed the box hedges trimmed back into shape. I don't like strictly-weeded paths, but I knifed out the dandelions that had wedged themselves between the flagstones, and encouraged stray seedlings of thyme, self heal and herb robert which wove their own sweet way between the cobbles.

All the while I was doing this I was thinking about the fourth quadrangle. On fine days after work I'd stand on the stony patch among the dockens, right at the middle of the fourth quadrangle, playing my flute. I was glad to be reunited with my flute after so long apart. I hadn't been sure I'd find it where I'd left it, but when I got home Phyllis had left a note on my door: "Don't take anything away. Rue will come back."

It took a while for my flute and I to get in tune with each other again. I started to pick up some pieces from the Nunks at Practice, and I listened, just as I used to do, to the Conductor's piano music coming from the upstairs window. I understood now why our Conductor never played at Practice. The Conductor has to weave all the different colours into the right pattern. On my travels I sometimes saw Conductors arrange the pattern and be one of the players at the same time. Our Conductor never does that, and our music is the purest I ever heard. Our Conductor has strong spectacles, a bent-over back and a shuffly walk these days, but the disembodied notes from the open window are more transcendent than ever. Transposing the Conductor's music to my flute is far more difficult than translating what I hear at Practice. I have to concentrate, and even now I never get it exactly right. I always end my playing with the same tune, one that Brother Anselm taught me right at the beginning. I play it every fine evening until the song thrush starts to echo the same tune back to me.

I spoke to Sister Angela about the fourth quadrangle one day when she was awake in the afternoon. On fine days I used to wheel her chair to the sunniest spots, the very ones where Cosette used to drag her bed as the sun wheeled round. Today Sister Angela was sitting by the door next to a pot of sweet peas, which I'd put there because they reminded me of Dorothy and her knitting at the House for Lost People.

"You're asking my advice?" Sister Angela sounded astonished. "Well, I'll say this, Rue, you're much chattier than you used to be, but I never thought the day would come when you asked me what I thought."

"I value your *opinion*," I said stiffly. I never appreciated personal remarks. It was only fair to add, "At the beginning, you taught me *everything*."

"Good to hear. I'm glad you noticed. Oh yes, I told you *things*. You always lapped up information, I'll say that for you. But opinions, no. You never asked for those."

"Suppose I'm asking you now?"

"I'll soon be dead," remarked Sister Angela inconsequentially. "You've made a garden for the living to rejoice in, which is a good thing. Life doesn't last long, and it's usually nothing to laugh about. You've given it a bit of colour. What about the soul?"

"The *soul?*"

"The immortal soul," said Sister Angela stoutly. "The fourth quadrangle is yours now, Rue. I've given it over. It's all yours."

Well, that flummoxed me. I had no idea what she meant. Dennis wasn't much more help. He answered my question with a question. "Where do the people go?"

"What people?"

"The people who come into the knot garden." I could tell he was trying to be patient. "Where do they sit?"

"In my way," I answered promptly. "They bring rugs and cushions. Sometimes even whole chairs. Like they *owned* the place."

"They do own it."

"What d'you mean? It's not *theirs*."

"Who owns anything?" said Dennis. "That's an old word you're using. You don't notice because it's a dead metaphor. See Jo there? He looks happy enough, lying there in the shade. Like he owns the place, you might say. In a manner of speaking, that is. That's all it is."

I carefully observed the next Supplicant who came into the knot garden, as if he were an inexplicably wilting plant. He was a tall thin man with the saddest face I've ever seen. A word came to me as I watched: *careworn*. I don't think I'd ever used that word in my thoughts before. I did something I'd never done before. I went and stood in front of him, my watering can hooked over my arm, and spoke: "Why do you come into the knot garden?"

His eyes were so weary they frightened me. He took a long time to answer. "For the peace," he said at last.

After that I left him in peace.

Basil visited us that winter. I was sweeping dead leaves off the paths when he came into the knot garden. It took me a minute to recognise him. There were lines on his face, and grey hairs at his temples. But his bright brown eyes were the same. I recalled the first time I'd looked into them, on a level with mine. To my horror he ran up and hugged me before I could slip aside. He smelt of autumn: wet leaves, apples and mud. Then the hug was over and I was able to take a deep breath.

While he was with us Basil and I spent a lot of time together. Basil talked about his travels, about the people he'd met along the way, and about the family he now had. It was like listening to the gentle babbling of a moorland stream. I imagined peat-brown water bordered with rush grass, cotton grass and dark green mosses. It occurred to me that Basil had always been kind, and now he was also wise. In due course I asked him about the fourth quadrangle.

"Solace," he said at once. "You know what the world out there is like, Rue. You know what people can do to each other. The good and the bad. It's a struggle. The fourth quadrangle – make it *kind*."

"But *I'm* not kind."

"I know you're not. Never were. But the knot garden isn't about *you*."

The soul is in the senses, which are all we have. I couldn't deal with anything immortal, whatever Sister Angela said. Even the rocks are not immortal. Instead I concentrated on solace for the senses, for all five of which the knot garden was now abundant. Warm in winter, cool in summer, pleasing curves for eye and foot to follow. The song of the blackbirds who nested in the sheltering hedge, our robin trilling out his territory, the song thrush tapping a snail against the stones. Low cooing of doves, and old Jo snoring in his patch of sun. Mingling scents of lavender, lilac and roses. The bittersweet smell of aubretia when you handle it. Sharpness of sorrel when you bite it, sweetness of coriander against the tongue: lovage, parsley, pungent chives. The feel of leaves under fingers, sharp-edged box, soft chicory, rough rosemary, velvety lavender pinched between fingers to get the scent. Colours of winter: blues, dark greens and greys. Yellow sparks in spring, then all the colours, not just red, ochre, orange and yellow, but also blues and greens and all the colours of the long-lost sea in one small enclosed inland garden. No need to leave it; everything in my whole world was here.

In the centre of the circle of benches at the heart of the fourth quadrangle I laid a slab of coarse-grained granite. The sunlight caught sparks of quartz and mica. In wet weather it was rough enough not to get slippery. Its colours changed with the weather and the seasons. Sometimes it was full of grey, and other times flecked with pink. It held the nearest I could get to 'immortal': a story I'd learned at school about fire and molten rock, a spinning planet slowly becoming itself, and just as slowly becoming something other, and other again, until it ceased to be itself any more, but all the little flecks would melt again and turn into something else. This would go on forever, though I didn't know exactly what forever meant. Maybe we'd done it in maths at school, but I couldn't remember all that now.

I made the path for the fourth quadrangle in a figure of eight, forever going round and round on itself. Bordered by hedges that were evergreen, the beds were a pattern of triangles with curved edges. I planted them with the kindliest plants I knew: southernwood and antique roses, and heartsease round the central circle.

When they come in the evenings – Nunks, Orphans, Providers and Supplicants – I bring out a little brazier and make a fire above the granite slab. The fire lights up their changing faces as they talk or sit there silently. Sometimes I look at the faces. Mostly I just leave them to it.

One day a skinny white-faced girl stood in my way as I was

leaving. I'd never seen her before, nor since. "I want to thank you," she said. "They told me you made all this."

I half nodded, not looking at her.

"Who are you?" she asked me. A strange question, but I wasn't angry. I felt as though I'd been waiting for it.

I told her my true name.

Next morning, just like every other morning, I put the brazier away and swept up the cold ash, leaving the granite bare once more. Then Jo and I fetched our tools, and I set to work again.

About the author

Margaret Elphinstone is the author of ten previous novels and two books on organic gardening. Her historical novels include *The Sea Road*, *Voyageurs*, *Light* and *The Gathering Night*. She really thought she would write no more novels, but then came *Lost People*.

https://www.margaretelphinstone.co.uk/

Praise for *Lost People*

Set in a future in which humans are tentatively rebuilding the idea of community after some unspecified global disaster, *Lost People* has a meditative, calming mood and pace despite the fact that things have gone so badly wrong. The writing is beautiful, especially the voice of Rue, the troubled, vulnerable, highly intelligent young person who tells the story. Margaret Elphinstone has created a world simultaneously strange and familiar. It is a novel unlike any I have read for some time.

James Robertson, poet and novelist

Here is a story of trauma, the kindness of strangers and the healing power of animals and plants. It may have happened aeons ago, or might be yet to come, or might even be occurring here and now. *Lost People* is a gem-like wisdom-tale of perfect clarity and depth.

Kathleen Jamie, Scotland's Makar

Lost People is a precious gift. It opens up sanctuaries and pathways through scented herb gardens, through by-ways of restoration for all who find themselves lost. To read *Lost People* is to trace the illuminations of a manuscript coming alive from its centuries sleeping, to be in a world of colour amidst destruction, to be reminded of the simple things that are part of the right to be ordinary, to be quiet, to find song. Once again Margaret Elphinstone has made worlds which never flinch from the consequences of war but help us find ways into the work of healing, peace and refuge.

Alison Phipps, UNESCO Chair for Refugee Integration through Languages and Arts at the University of Glasgow

A timeless, mesmerising jewel of a story, balm for the soul.
Mandy Haggith, novelist and poet

Timeless yet immediate, a haunting fable rooted in reality, Margaret Elphinstone's visionary writing creates an adjacent world to our present plagues of war, and societal dislocation. Yet within her poetic meditation, as rooted in the healing herbs of her novel's knot garden, also sprouts a harvest of hope, and the potential for redemption. This is a story of lyrical urgency, beautifully told; gift, adventure and manifesto from a writer of wonders and lament.
Martyn Halsall, poet and journalist

The book is beautifully written, and the author's humanity shines through it very clearly, as does her knowledge of gardens and plants. There's a clarity of expression in the narrative which makes it easy to read, and yet there are layers of meaning within it. Very satisfying.
Colin Will, poet

Wild Goose Publications, the publishing house of the Iona Community established in the Celtic Christian tradition of Saint Columba, produces books, e-books, CDs and digital downloads on:

- holistic spirituality
- social justice
- political and peace issues
- healing
- innovative approaches to worship
- song in worship, including the work of the Wild Goose Resource Group
- material for meditation and reflection

Visit our website at
www.ionabooks.com
for details of all our products and online sales